"A powerful and quirky nove[...] *of the Homeless* reads like what might happen if you grafted the Swans's *To Be Kind* to a Barry Hannah tree and then picked whatever fruit grew from it and made a smoothie out of it."
— Brian Evenson, author of *A Collapse of Horses* and *Last Days*

"G. Arthur Brown is at the forefront of a new generation of writers. One of my favorites."
— Brian Keene, best-selling author of *The Complex*

"G. Arthur Brown—already respected as a syntactically immaculate weaver of words both comical and absurd— now ventures into the darkness to deliver us the strange and unsettling horrors of *Governor of the Homeless*."
— Jeremy Robert Johnson, author of *Skullcrack City*

"G. Arthur Brown's work is so far removed from what everyone else is doing that we need new words to describe it. Bum Town is full of weird noir, bizarro, science fiction, surreal madness, and elegant absurdity. This is beautiful prose wrapped in uncertainty and mystery. Whatever genre you like, Brown is using it in his mix and then turning it into pretzels that eat you and make you like it." — Gabino Iglesias, author of *Zero Saints*

"We're in Bum Town, a fully realized cartoonish dystopia the likes of which you'd find in a Terry Gilliam film, and the world presented felt SO alive to me that I feel like there's 100's of more stories this place has to tell. This is an impressive feat for a novella..." — Danger Slater, author of *Puppet Skin*

"It's a story of insanity. Or, several stories of insanities. Twisting in on each other, folding out from each other, an Escher print made from words." — Christine Morgan, The Horror Fiction Review

"G. Arthur Brown is a glorious minstrel making music for demon gods to dance to. His prose is taut, charming, and sinister. His mind quick, quirky, and wild. Let the moon go up at midnight and let him serenade you. Open up your heart at him: let his stories make you full." — Brian Allen Carr, author of *The Last Horror Novel in the History of the World*

"I think this book ate holes in my brain. G. Arthur Brown is a magician of absurd stories and surreal imagery." — CV Hunt, author of *Ritualistic Human Sacrifice*

"Reading this requires a complete detachment from reality..." — Pedro Proença, author of *Benjamin*

"G. Arthur Brown writes with the chittering sing-song staccato of a filthy street urchin in an accent that might be Cock-knee but actually it's something else you should probably recognize but don't due to the plastic dry-cleaning bag over his head." — Arthur Graham, author of *Editorial*

"It's been a couple years since the publication of G Arthur Brown's impressive debut novella, *Kitten*, but who's counting? With *Governor of the Homeless*—the author's second long-form work to see publication and the inaugural offering of small press newcomer Psychedelic Horror Press—Brown dodges the sophomore slump with a novella that is as singularly dark, weird, and thought-provoking as it is skillfully written." — Douglas Hackle, author of *The Hottest Gay Man Ever Killed in a Shark Attack*

"*Governor of the Homeless* is the size of a tapas, but it's got striking flavors of big, bold tomes like *Infinite Jest*, *1984*, and *White Noise*. This book is smart, sharp, cracked, crazy. It smells like the randoms in the alley behind my apartment building digging through the bins, it's ugly like bloody gums, and it's funny like the punchline to your favorite joke." — Laura Lee Bahr, author of *Haunt*

"Myriad narratives spiral out from a central courtroom drama. The sum of the parts: a portal into the mind of the author, a kind of twisted dream diary, a nightmare of Baudrillard's simulacra, wrought with exquisite detail" — Jason Rizos, author of *Supercenter*

"Kaleidoscopic weirdness flows unabated, and the imagery washing past is disturbing and psychedelic. The text is experiential and striking, but lacking in concrete handholds beyond a few grotesque set pieces." — Ross E. Lockhart, Editor in Chief of Word Horde

Psychedelic Horror Press
Virginia, USA

www.psychedelichorrorpress.com
psychedelichorrorpress@gmail.com

Interior Design by Nicholaus Patnaude
Interior Illustraions by Sarah Kushwara
artbysarahkushwara.tumblr.com

ISBN 978-0-578-18522-4

First Edition

PHP - 001

Governor
of the
Homeless

by
G. Arthur Brown

Table of Contents:

1

On a street corner Wilson found the Governor of the Homeless panhandling. The man's attire did not give him away. In fact, he denied that he held any office whatsoever. He appeared to be the same as any other bum. But it had to be the Governor; Wilson believed he had a knack for knowing these things.

Wilson waited and the city sky smeared from clear blue to simple gray to hazy brown born of the contamination of street lights. He watched his quarry all the while, until such time as the Governor took his small dog, Beyonce, in hand and put his collection of garbage in an old shopping cart, and then moved from his corner into an alleyway that no one but cats and vagrants traversed.

Wilson buttoned his trench coat, pulled up his collar for courage, and became the Governor's shadow. He felt his

snub-nose in his pocket. He lumbered taller than his five feet, four inches should have allowed. He wore dark glasses despite the lack of sun. He had shaved his head but not his face earlier in the day. The stubble, the coat, the shades, the black porkpie hat: he was a specter. The Governor didn't know what was coming for him. When we asked him about it later, Wilson insisted he had transformed during the incident. He looked at the security camera pictures and could not identify himself, unlike half a dozen eyewitnesses. His detailed recollections had some glaring gaps.

The first thing Wilson saw in the alley, according to later testimony, was the facedown body of a naked female he referred to as "The Angel." Her feathers had been plucked, but he could see her embarrassed chicken wings, curled up as if to avoid detection. He examined them and made a quick note on his pad about the scaly texture. This was introduced later as Exhibit G. The judge almost laughed when the defense team presented this in open court. I was certainly shocked and didn't know what to make of it at the time.

After he left The Angel, Wilson moved further into the alley, which became a labyrinth full of shanties and false walls that obscured God knows what. If he'd had more time, he would have busted them down and exposed their inhabitants or the troves of arcane relics they concealed. At the torn corner of a sheet hiding an opening into a disused tenement, he observed a pile of hands: all left hands of wizards, he later claimed. He was torn apart on cross examination because there was no way he could confirm that they were all left hands.

Wilson pushed on, for he still sought the Governor who was nearly out of sight, escaping into foreboding shadows. He was able to gain a small amount of ground before he noticed the screaming. It was not, he said, the screaming of mortals. No one in the courtroom was at all surprised by that remark, not even the more skittish members of the jury who shuddered every time the prosecutor ruffled his wig. Wilson

3

went on, saying that the scream was female, ghostly, an omen of ill fate. I wonder now why he did not heed that omen. His actions afterwards seem almost childishly reckless upon reflection.

It was obvious to me that Wilson was insane, and this was hardly surprising given the composition of Bum Town: the mad, the forgotten, the unclean. I cannot fault him for losing his grip on reality, for what is reality if not a consistent adherence to rules? Rules do not apply in Bum Town. Sane truth must be observed by a conforming society. Bum Town is anything but. Ask me, next time you see me, how I came to Bum Town and maybe I will tell you a long, meandering tale that may not have anything to do with sane truth. I can only offer you my word that what I say really happened somewhere, at some time, to someone who used to be or who would become me.

But I think I was talking about Wilson.

The first time I met Wilson, I was pretending to be a lookout for a dice game. Not craps, no one has any taste for that game anymore. It was something that Chinese Charlie had devised, something similar to Mah-Jong. The numbers all represented flowers and Oriental mystical symbols. Box cars won you an egg roll if Chinese Charlie had one on him. Wilson was pretending he was interested in getting a place in the game, but I already knew he was trying to sniff out information. He couldn't wait to start asking questions about the Governor. Our first conversation went something like this:

Wilson: Hey, hey. You running this game?

Me: No way. Charlie runs these games. Chinese Charlie.

Wilson: He doesn't look Chinese.

Me: He's probably not. And I doubt his name is really Charlie.

Wilson: Charles, then, most likely.

Me: Not even. It's something with an A.

Wilson: Charles does have an A.

Me: Are you in or are you out?

Wilson: (Handing me a five) I am in. Oh, hey, buddy. Do you know anything about who runs Bum Town?

From there he proceeded to not-so-subtly schmooze with all the other players, tossing out some of his theories about the Governor and opinions on his policies about the future security of Bum Town and the use of a nonhuman police force. His eyes were not clear, not sharp with the look of a man bent on murder. I don't know if he had convinced himself at that point that the Governor needed to pay for Dr. Chalupnik's sins. Wilson didn't make that clear in what testimony he was able to give. But he already hated Chalupnik. I remember him saying so as he left the game. Something like, "Fuck! I'm all out of dough. Oh, well, at least I have my hatred for that shitbird Doctor C." (Doctor C., he admitted on the stand, was a nickname for Chalupnik.) Though, if I'm to be honest, Wilson sounded more like he was reading that crap off a script than speaking from his gut.

The lunatic Wilson was on trial for killing the Governor of the Homeless, but we all knew he hadn't. The Governor was alive and sitting in the courtroom. Only Wilson believed he had killed the Governor. This trial was about something else entirely. I'm writing this to see if I can figure out what that was.

2

There was another time Wilson came around sniffing at the dice game, a lot later. It was drizzling that night, little bullseyes in the reflections of a neon sign on the cracked sidewalk. Wilson tromped right through that puddle like he didn't give a shit about having wet feet. And he was as subtle as last time:

Wilson: Hey, friend. I can't stay away. Got money to lose. Burning a hole in my pocket.

Me: Well, walk through a deeper puddle and that fire will go right out.

Wilson: I didn't know you were funny.

Me: I don't feel funny. I feel wet. You in?

Wilson: (Handing me a five) Yeah, friend, of course. So Charlie ain't Chinese, is he?

Me: You're like a broken record. He ain't Chinese, no. I don't think so.

Wilson: What is he then?

Me: Shit, Black and Vietnamese I think.

Wilson: No shit?

Me: I don't know. He's the boss. He runs the game. Why do you care?

Wilson: Just curious, friend.

Me: Why don't you ask him? Charlie.

Charlie comes over.

Me: This boot-nugget wants to know your freaking ancestry.

Charlie: Why? Am I inheriting money? Tell me I got a rich uncle that died with no direct heirs and you'll make me one happy motherfucker.

Me: Nah, he wants to know your race.

Charlie: (Stares at Wilson) That right? You a racist, man?

Wilson: No. No way. (Averting his eyes.)

Charlie: Coon, Spic, and Chink with a little Kraut and Mick way back in the woodpile. Got a problem with that?

Wilson looked scared for a minute. Then he laughed nervously. Charlie patted him on the back, waved him in and they went to play the game.

That was a weird night, if I'm recalling the correct night, because that's the night that a couple of Arboghasts showed up. Their gasmasks tight on their faces, they spoke in the clipped, mechanical tones that we all were familiar with but could never understand. They wore that red leather, dyed in blood some said, so tight and all over, which gave rise to the rumors that they were, in fact, made of leather, hollow on the inside or some gears or baby organs preserved in the amnion of a woman carrying a demon-seed. They had one of those clockwork vultures with them on a long chain. Its skeletal face stared at me but I couldn't be sure if it was seeing me, with the severe lack of eyes in the orbits.

At first I assumed the Arboghasts were going to break up the game, some new ruling from the Governor's Office. But they sort of watched the fellows play and whisper-clicked asides to one another while they fed dead snakes to their pet. It made everybody pretty nervous to have them just hanging around, and you could hardly blame the rowdies playing that night, because you usually didn't see any Arboghasts unless they were out breaking heads and taking ears and fingers and foreskins as trophies.

When the game started to wind down, Wilson broke off rather quickly, and the Arboghasts took note of that, though they didn't pursue. It could have been they put one of their tracking slugs on him to catch up to him later.

And then the mekanik carrion bird started making this horrible squawking that filled all our souls with visions

of large, dingy bodies of water full of leviathans ready to rise up and eat us like we were grapes wearing dirty clothes. The rest of the boys shuffled off and Charlie glared at those two Arboghasts.

One chirped to the other, and they busted out in their stale, cardboard version of laughter, finally drifting back out into the night to wherever it is those things go.

I said to Charlie:

Me: You see them 'ghasts, huh?

Charlie: Course I saw them. Whatchoo think, I'm blind? They fucked up the game tonight. Taking the piss out of my wind.

Me: I think they were here for the weirdo. The one who was asking about you and the Governor.

Charlie: Man, I don't know nothing about nothing. They could have just been out for some fun. Arboghasts might like fun, right? No reason why they couldn't.

Me: If they wanted fun they'd have joined in the game.

Charlie: Maybe nervous. Never actually played before. Don't wanna make fools of theyselfs so they was just observing.

Me: Maybe.

Charlie: Man, as long as they wasn't clubbing in the heads of the players, that's good enough for me. I guess I'm going home, to bed.

That was the last time I saw Charlie in human form.

3

Amongst Wilson's possessions, when they tossed his room in the flophouse, was a dime-store paperback called *Abortionstein*. The book is the story of a female detective on the trail of a sadistic murderer who has been dumping the corpses of prostitutes with aborted fetuses sewn into their wombs.

Meanwhile, small, deformed children have been showing up around town, on playgrounds, etc., attacking pets and regular children. One feature ties them together: they all have cat eyes. An ancient Shawnee legend says that children with cat eyes are soulless abominations. Somehow, for no explained reason, the DNA of one of these creatures is tested and tied to a woman in town who confesses to having had an abortion in the recent past. She had been raped. An ancient Iroquois legend says that rape babies are soulless.

It becomes clear to the detective that this is the work of a madman obsessed with "reversing" the abortion procedure. He is sewing the dead fetal tissue back into the womb in hopes of breathing life back into it. Instead, the whores he has kidnapped become incredibly sick and die. But for some reason, rape babies are being "carried to term"—being revived as monsters. He wants to create healthy, normal, non-rape babies. The man is maddened by this failure.

The reverse abortions also garner the attentions of a televangelist in the area on a Pro-Life crusade. The evangelist mistakes the handiwork of this butcher as the attempt to fulfill the will of God, so he hires a private investigator to track the man down. Once he has discovered the doctor's lair, the evangelist sneaks in to marvel at the wonders that God has wrought by the hands of this man the media has dubbed Abortionstein. He finds a cage full of the cat-eyed children, and he releases them, thinking they are miracles. They tear the man to pieces and drink his blood.

The detective follows the evangelist and falls right into Abortionstein's trap. Dr. Chalpuniak, the man dubbed Abortionstein, blames his failures on the dirty wombs of the prostitutes he used as his initial subjects. He needs a clean womb, the womb of the detective, a chaste woman who has never known a man, or at least this is what Chalpuniak believes.

A wealthy eccentric who enjoys dining on fetuses ransacks Abortionstein's lair. Luckily for the detective, he stumbles upon her tied up to a table while Abortionstein is in another room. He frees her, and they rig up some dynamite and blow up the lair. We are supposed to assume Abortionstein is killed in the explosion, but then at the very end his hand pokes out of the rubble, with bits of aborted baby stitched in with his normal flesh, suggesting a sequel.

There was no such sequel. But there was a brief listing of other works available by the author that included *Chalupacabra*, *Atomic Dinosaur Manchild*, and *One Light Year and 50 Million Kill-o-Watt Hours from Earth*. These books were not found among Wilson's possessions.

4

When Wilson was cross-examined on the stand, which consisted of little more than some old orange crates, he said he had originally been hired by Dr. Chalupnik six years ago. At first he did not understand the true nature of the man's work, but it quickly became apparent that Dr. C was not your run of the mill witchdoctor. He had some kind of laboratory hooked up, full of Tesla coils, theremins, and Van de Graaff generators. "That wasn't stuff you used for herbalism, not even in this modern age of technology," Wilson claimed.

The prosecutor, scratching the mop head he wore as a wig, asked if Dr. Chalupnik ever told Wilson he was an herbalist, and Wilson said he had not. He claimed to have never asked the man what kind of work he did or what the devices were for. This made no sense, and the prosecutor could barely contain his laughter when he asked Wilson, "How can you take a job where you don't know what's going on?" And everyone in the room burst out laughing.

Wilson said, barely loud enough to hear, "Ask anyone in government." But the remark was stricken from the record.

I think it was obvious at this point to everyone in that squalid cellar chamber courtroom that Wilson was a certifiable head case, but who in Bum Town was not? I started working on an old connect-the-dots I'd found in an abandoned stroller. I can't be sure if what I heard next was something I imagined or not. I seem to recall that Wilson screamed, not the scream of a grown man, but the gurgling cry of a newborn infant. It got louder and louder, but I was intent on working on the puzzle, because these dots were pretty hard to connect. The judge ordered an au pair, or at least a girl who did not speak a lot of English, to tend to Wilson, to get him back in sorts so the questioning could continue. A kid in the gallery had an old pink Walkman hooked to chintzy little computer speakers and she was playing a garbled version of "Lovely Day" by Bill Withers. The judge ordered her to turn it up and claimed this was "his jam." A few drifters in the back danced while a hag in front of me got out of her seat to vomit into one of the buckets placed in the cobwebbed corners.

A calm descended over the rabble gathered in the dank gallery, and people retook their seats upon old church pews salvaged from a burnt chapel. Wilson stopped screaming at some point and had already resumed responding normally, or as close to normal as could be expected from a nuthatch like that. He was now detailing his problem with the Street Cleaners, who, he claimed, were eating our brethren in the City proper if they should be caught out after curfew. In his mind they were specially bred cannibalistic mutants who dined on the street trash, living and dead. The city kept them locked up in the daylight far from the prying eyes of the decent citizenry.

Could he have been correct? I had no idea. We all knew

that bums weren't safe outside Bum Town, and given that we had something as heinous as Arboghasts prowling our streets, it seemed plausible that the City could have monstrous Street Cleaners out and about after the sun goes down.

The judge ordered him to move on. This testimony had nothing to do with the question asked. The Street Cleaners were in no way tied to either Dr. C. or to the Governor, and so the thin, white-haired child was released from within the judge's robe. It scurried up to the stand and began whacking Wilson on his legs and arms with a rattan baton.

The defense objected to the flogging.

The judge agreed to put a nickel into the Injustice Jar, an old plastic mayonnaise container that he chucked a coin in whenever he violated due process. The jar was looking quite full, and it had been empty when court took session that morning.

Wilson requested a consult with his sponsor.

The court was briefly adjourned.

I went outside for a smoke and a stroll.

I saw Filthy Grey Hawkins out there in a shopping cart-littered street. He had two strings on his rectangular body guitar. "I invented this here guitar," he always claimed. "Bo Diddley done stole it up!" Filthy was only about three decades younger than Diddley, though he looked every bit of a hundred years old. His gnarled fingers glided over the guitar frets sublimely, and he could play any variety of blues or ragtime you might want to hear, or not want to hear if your tastes were more like mine.

Me: Why'ontcha give that thing a rest, Filthy?

Filthy: I let it rest, I might as well just curl up in a ball and die. My soul is the sound coming out this guitar rye-chere. Thoe me one them empty bottles for a slide.

Me: I don't know how you make any kind of sensible songs on there without the strings.

Filthy: Two is more than enough. I do more on these two than that hack Hendrix did on six. And I ain't gotta cheat and play all left-handed.

I gave him the bottle, and he made those dual wires buzz with a song that could make a certain type of person cry. But I am not that type of person. I don't care for the blues.

A yappy stray dog came up to us, barking especially at Filthy. I told it to shush. Filthy kept on playing, acting like the dog was singing along with him. I was about to run the noisy beast off when I saw the shadowy form of something buzzard-like ooze from the sky down onto the little barking thing. It grabbed the dog's hind quarters in its talons and decapitated the mutt with its metal beak. The vultures usually don't sic live quarry without a command from their Arboghast handlers. I thought maybe it smelled the stink coming off Filthy and mistook it for the odor of carrion.

Me: That wasn't your dog, was it?

Filthy: No. No, man. But it ain't deserve to go out like that. That ain't right!

Me: Yeah, bothers me that I don't see this bird's keeper anywhere around.

Filthy: Can they get free? Turn all feral?

Me: I guess that's possible. Happens a lot in old sci-fi movies.

Filthy: It's a lot scurrier in real life.

Me: Yeah.

Then the thing flew away with what little remained of the dog in its grip.

5

Somehow I was able to get ahold of evidence from the case. A few dozen pages of a typewritten manuscript for something called *Clean Streets*, presumably written by Wilson. It read like a pulp novel, though it was supposedly a historical novel based on rigorous research of the present era. This seemed to imply that he thought everything he had made up on the page was a reflection of reality.

It was clear at this point that Wilson's thinking was deranged. Somehow he'd become convinced there were large flesh-eating monsters loose in the city to purge it of undesirables—that this was a plan put into action by some municipal committee for the improvement of the community. It was far-fetched, but there was something compelling in the earnestness of the prose that troubled me more so than the fact Wilson had put a slug in the back of some poor bastard's head thinking he was the Governor. It's one thing to kill a man; it's quite another to concoct some kind of reality on the page that deliberately twists and perverts a man's mind.

The story followed a cast of sympathetic characters, including the obligatory shot-gun-wielding man of action, a mentally impaired maiden fair, two young boys with filthy striped shirts, one of the handlers of the Street Cleaners themselves who was quite conflicted about her job, and a corrupt cop who winds up killing everybody at the end. (The last two pages of the story were included with the others.)

A few of the passages return to me every once in a while. They've pushed out my own pri-vate daydreams with this half-dystopian, half-romanticized doom. Sometimes I see a kid staggering along some side street, and he's wearing a striped shirt, and it's filthy. And I just lose it. I just break down right there, weeping like a baby for the childhood I lost in the fire.

They burned my fucking brain. Not a lot of people can say that.

6

One time Wilson brought his girlfriend to the dice game. She was missing an arm but was otherwise pretty attractive in an alley cat sort of way. Red hair, the color of spray paint. Smokey eyes from the fact she never removed her makeup. She'd led a hard life—you could see that. But you could also see she knew how to have a good time, which made it puzzling why she'd be with Wilson, who was the place you go to stare into the internal void of tedious existence. He was a stick in the mud, a wet blanket, a killjoy, a party pooper, and a spoilsport. Sometimes all at once.

As the game progressed, this girl wandered off into

alcoves with a couple different guys under the pretext that they were going to smoke. Everyone shooting dice was already smoking, so I figured she must be hooking. A handy or a blow-jay for some of the fellas to put a little bit of coin in Wilson's pocket to waste on the game.

Later, when I talked with the guys she'd gone off with, they said she was giving it away for free, but she kept asking a bunch of questions about the Governor and Bum Town, asking if they knew Chalupnik or anything about the Street Cleaners.

So Wilson must've hired her to try to get tongues wagging by getting cocks throbbing. None of the guys had any useful information though, and most had at least gonorrhea.

Meanwhile, Wilson was standing by, betting just enough to make it look as if he were interested in the game.

"You know people used to be able to fly in the pre-historic times," he said out of nowhere while the girl was off reconnoitering.

"That's bullshit," Charlie said. A bunch of the others laughed. We didn't know what he was talking about.

"It's true. People now only use about ten percent of their brain. In those days, they used pretty much the whole thing. And they could fly."

I thought he meant psychic powers, but he went on: "They used their huge brains—because they had those big foreheads so their brains were bigger—they used those brains to figure out how to saddle up pteranodons and fly those bug-gers around the sky."

Kep, the old card sharp, squinted and bared his four teeth, and asked, "What the fuck a terranondon?"

Wilson, very seriously, elucidated: "The media com-monly refer to all flying reptiles of the dinosaur era—and they are not dinosaurs—as pterodactyls. But those are only one spe-cific type of pterosaur, like their distant cousins the pterano-dons."

"So, flying dinosaurs?" asked Rip Ravel, a legally blind ex-trucker.

"Well, they are not technically dinosaurs, but the media call them that."

"So, what is they?" Kep said. "Dragons?"

Wilson's eyes went narrow, in rage or disgust, I couldn't tell. "If you can't figure out what I'm talking about, I'm done here," he said, and went quiet.

And I looked up into the grimy night sky there, and in the moonlight I could sort of make out the silhouette of a giant bird. Was it a bird? Was it an Arboghast on some clock-work vulture big enough to ride? Was it a genius caveman on a pterodactyl ?

Was it a dragon?

Theory I heard was that dinosaurs never actually died out. They simply evolved over time into other things, basilisks and wyverns. Or maybe just birds. But here's the interesting thing: when I was in school they showed us all these pictures of this thing called Archaeopteryx. Sort of a lizard with feathery wings. Now, they told us that it couldn't actually fly, but it could glide. How they knew this, I'm not sure. Not like they had the Zapruder footage of Wilbur and Orville Archaeopteryx trying to get off the ground. And they said that, over time, this monster gave birth to another monster that was slightly more like a bird until, eventually, they actually could fly. And then all birds came out of that, even the ones that don't fly. They lost that gift somewhere down the line.

Years later, I saw a book that said Archaeopteryx was an evolutionary dead end, but he had a cousin who was similar, and the cousin was the one who fathered all of birdkind. But the thing is: this cousin was only theorized to exist. They didn't actually have the fossils to prove it, but he had to exist because their theory was sound. It couldn't have happened any other way. They wouldn't have come up with this model if it wasn't the best one.

Archaeopteryx, in case you are getting any zany thoughts, was way too small to ride even if it could fly. You might be able to tape a gerbil to its back. Just for the sake of science.

Kep laughed at Wilson, drawing me out of my reverie. Wilson was more or less pouting. "This fool think he's a prophet of science or some shit."

"Now that you mention it," Wilson said, "I do have a prediction about the future of science." He seemed to be re-engaged, enthusiastic again.

"Oh, yeah, professor?" joked Chinese Charlie. "Why don't you remove the blinkers of ignorance from our fucking eyes"—he pretended to pull away a blindfold and see for the first time—"and enlighten us?"

Wilson looked like he didn't even hear the mocking tone in the men's voices. He puffed himself up a bit, ready to impart some really valuable bit of wisdom to younger siblings. Or like he was about to tell a really scary story around the campfire.

"You know how technology has gotten smaller? In the 50s computers used to take up an entire room. By the 80s a computer could fit on your desktop and had more power than all those reel to reel monsters you see in the old movies. In the 70s calculators sat on your desk. By the 80s they could fit in your pocket. The trend is for technology to get smaller and smaller. Now people have computers they refer to as phones that have more power than all the computers that existed in the 80s put together."

Kep nodded, looking surprised. "Yep. That's true. What comes next?"

"In the future," Wilson continued, "maybe sixty years from now, maybe eighty, things will get so small that people can no longer use them. It's the singularity that many have predicted. Total power in our technology, but far more miniscule than any human can make use of. So we return to the Dark

30

Ages, as barbarians, barely able to remember what pencils are for."

"Fuck, you talkin' Mad Max? Road Warrior?" Rip Ravel asked with a raucous snort.

"Oh, shit! I'm all about some post-apocalyptic barbarian action!" Charlie said, giving high fives to Kep and Rip, but Wilson left him hanging.

"It's not going to be a fun time, gents. It's going to be the end," Wilson said.

The end. Like Archaeopteryx, I wondered? We die while our weird cousins go on to evolve small enough to operate the teeny-tiny gizmos the future holds. Freaking gremlins inside the gears and mechanisms or, what do they have now, diodes and capacitors? Small enough to wander around inside the fiber optic cables. Small enough to inhabit the empty spaces between electrons and nuclei. Really fucking itty-bitty. Possibly giving new meaning to 'quantum mechanics.' They could be in there, in the future, tinkering with the positions of subatomic particles with minute wrenches they pull from their teensy tool belts.

Or, maybe Wilson is a lunatic who doesn't know what he's talking about. Still, if he's led me to a dead end, there's got to be some way of getting to point B from point A. You can always get there from here.

7

When younger guys, still green behind the ears, who look up to me ask me if I've seen much action, I have a favorite story I always enjoy telling. I tell them, one night I was out on the streets, not in a capacity as an enforcer—I had the night off. But I was packing a Desert Eagle tucked into my waistband.

Two Arboghasts rolled up the street. Both in tight, shiny, brand-new-looking red leather. They were outfitted with some new gadgetry that I'd never even seen before. I knew they had to be there hunting. The slightly taller one gurgled loudly and pointed down to the far end of the street.

I turned to look and saw only another Arboghast. This

one was thicker, like he'd been packed full of loose sausage almost to the point of bursting his darker, stained leathers. He was covered in long spikes, not the studs you see on young kids who want to play at being tough or goth or whathaveyou. These things were as sharp as pitchfork tines and almost as long. He was a throbbing porcupine stuck inside a slick jumpsuit. Holes in his false skin showed the metal-rod *bones* that truly composed these automata. He lurched forward at an alarming rate. I had no idea what was going on.

It was mere seconds before this larger Arboghast was upon the two smaller, newer models. The rending and shredding commenced, and though the big guy's condition made him more vulnerable, he moved with such deadly cunning that the other two could not gain a sufficient grip upon him to work free his boney infrastructure.

He ripped them, colloquially, new assholes—all over their bodies. He pulled out metal rods and things that looked as if they were once alive, all of which he discarded as so much rubbish on the street there and in the gutters.

What could it mean? Warring factions? A struggle for who would control Bum Town?

The big one snapped the final brittle remnants of the others and scattered bits of the carcasses with the fervor of a cage-raised fighting dog. And then he came right up to me.

He looked at me with his dead eyes. I saw my pitiful, shocked reflection in the black glass of his welder's goggles. I didn't shit my pants, and I wondered in the moment how anyone could shit themselves in this kind of situation. I had the opposite reaction: a clenching of all my body's sphincters. I couldn't have relieved myself if I'd tried. I'm shit-shy, I guess. But even without soiling myself, I knew terror in that moment. The embodiment of death and judgment and insanity right there glaring at me.

But—and this is the part that really impresses most people—I reached out my bare hand and I swatted him on the muzzle.

He jerked his head side to side in confusion, letting out a squeal that released a reddish smoke from a narrow slit in his tree-trunk of a neck. Verminous things leaked from his snapping maw. It bounced back from me, like an ape, sizing me up.

And then he huffed and turned and stalked off.

That's one version of the story. Truthfully, I can't remember which version is correct but I don't think it matters.

The other version sounds awfully similar to a passage from a book that I'm pretty sure I didn't write, causing me to wonder how it snuck into my life.

In this version, I'm at the very edge of Bum Town where it meets the old City. The two young Arboghasts are guarding Bum Town, I think. And a Street Cleaner charges them—somehow the invisible fence has failed and he's loose. I should be panicking but I'm just standing there, watching the fight. He's a head and half taller than either of those 'ghasts. He's nothing I've ever seen. He's got a prehensile tail that he uses to pull off one of their heads. It pops like a cork from a bottle of champagne, and the thing's vital essence sluices out like molasses full of cigarette butts and maggots.

He's just doing his job. I can't blame him. If the Arboghasts are anything, they are filth. And they need to be cleaned.

Anyway, there's another possible version of this story, which is that it didn't ever happen at all. It's the least impressive variation so I generally do not put this one forward first. If I did, I would sound the same as Brownhouse Petey. He used to say stuff like "One time nothing happened." He was a lunatic. Now he's dead. Now nothing happens to him all the time.

8

Wilson's trial reconvened. He was led back into the court room, head now shaved, hands bound with hog wire. The words *slave* and *garbage* had been carved with a razor into his arms. He wore a look of bemusement on his face, like a guy who recently got a heavy dose of toxic shock treatment. It appeared they had taught him a lesson that stuck.

"Can you tell us your name?" asked the prosecutor.

"Yes," Wilson said, staring down at his feet.

The prosecutor laughed and the defense attorney joined him.

"Okay, Mr. Wilson...where were we?" the prosecutor

said, putting his finger to his chin and staring at the ceiling histrionically.

"In an old boiler room that had been converted to a torture chamber," Wilson answered flatly.

"Good Lord, man! I didn't mean a literal location! I'm talking about where I left off with the questioning."

"You were asking me about Chalupnik."

"Yes, yes, I was. *Good doggie!*" He reached out to scratch Wilson's bald head.

The courtroom erupted in catcalls, guffaws, and jeering.

The judge quieted the court by hammering a finishing nail into the pile of debris that passed as his bench.

"That's enough of that for now. Save some for later, when his goose is really cooked."

"Where," asked the pacing lawyer, "did you first meet Dr. Chalupnik?"

Wilson looked at the judge and then at the jury.

"I... It was at a party. A soiree at the Governor's mansion."

"Do you expect us to believe that a dignitary such as the Governor would allow a piece of garbage like you into the midst of his echelon?"

"I was incognito."

"So you went there under false pretenses?"

"At the time," Wilson said lucidly, "I was just another loyal admirer of what I saw as a great man, a visionary, a leader. I had no idea what he was capable of at that point."

"So you went there under true pretenses?"

"I went there, pretense or no."

"And did the Governor himself introduce you to Dr. Chalupnik?"

"No, I was introduced to Dr. C. by a woman who brewed beer for the Governor."

"Did you see Dr. Chalupnik and the Governor converse at any point?"

"I don't believe so," Wilson said, grimacing. "I'm not entirely clear."

"In that case, please enlighten the court as to the connection between those two gentlemen."

Wilson coughed, trying to stall. "Dr. C. told me on at least two occasions that he was working directly under the Governor."

"So based on the word of a madman," said the prosecutor, "whom you claim to not even know what sort of work he did, you decided that the Governor was thereby responsible for the reverse-abortion experiments?"

Where was he going with this? What was the point of this line of questioning? It would seem long overdue to let the poor schmuck off the hook, tell him the Governor was not dead. The man he had killed was a nobody and he'd only get a slap on the wrist for not seeking permission before he took him out.

I still had no idea what was going on here. Was it all playacting for Wilson's torment? This had gone way too far. Perhaps it was playacting, but for the benefit of some other audience. The gallery, the bystanders, the rest of Bum Town.

A psychodrama reinforcing how important the Governor truly was.

And it was certainly no secret that the role and efficacy of the Governor had long been in question, gossip drifting glibly from lip to lip among the denizens of this forgotten district as they gambled, groused, and glommed on to anything that brought them a little sense of control. Knowing your place in the universe, even one as chaotic as Bum Town, was still an essential part of the man-bum psyche. I like to know where I stand, and who not to stand too close to. In Bum Town there are more reasons to keep your distance than just the stench, because everything stinks pretty equally. That's just a trick. A trick of the nose to keep you smell-blind to the real soul sharks, perched delicately on the psychic shoreline, exactly where ether meets the meat.

Somewhere outside I heard glass smashing. I heard a squeal that could only come from one of those mechanical carrion birds. The Arboghast bailiff started clapping, encouraging the court to join him. And he slipped over and pulled down the projector screen. The room went dark and an old movie flickered to life.

9

Black and white, or not quite—sepia tone, maybe. Filmed in the days of early talkies, or at least in that style. It's a Robin Hood movie, or something taking place in the Crusades, or sword and sorcery. I'm not sure it matters. The dialogue is stilted, sort of like a half-wit trying to sound like Shakespeare, but sounding more like Dickens, who, I'm pretty sure, never swung a sword in his life. Dickens, if he was ten and American and wrote Christmas pageants for local performance. The backdrop appears to be a castle of cardboard. Fanfare erupts, triumphant and bombastic.

There's a guy, about forty, with a bushy mustache. He's

in plate armor, with a chain coif on his head. A broad sword in his hand. His coat of arms as seen on his gamberson depicts a horse with a lion head. There is no name for the creature in any known lore; I looked it up later. This man is, I am willing to bet, a knight.

There's a woman, about twenty-five, with long blonde hair. She's wearing a dirty peasant dress, but her hair and make-up are perfect. She's attractive after a Northern European idealist fashion. I'm willing to bet she was a name that men knew in her day; her picture tacked to the wall in the pool hall or garage. She has a tattoo of the same nameless lion-horse on her left cheek.

"Lo, it has been quite a time at the wars! Now ten years agone I left thee as but a child with her daisy chains! All anon I love thee, Shandandra. Take the finger bones of my enemies as a token of my chivalrous affections." He pulls out a sack about the size of a human head and dumps the phalanges into her lap. She bundles them up in her skirts and giggles.

"Alack, I should have deigned to deliver ruth unto the wretches, the infidels. Peradventure, I could have made friends out of them after only a sound beating about the head and chest with my mace. Alas, 'twas not to be. Soothly, I preferred to cut off the fingers and save their bones as a trophy for my future wife."

"Future wife?" says the girl, batting her eyes.

"Why yes, Shandandra. My future wife," says the knight, leaning his head toward hers, placing his hand softly upon her chin, pressing the button that causes her face plate to detach. He rips her dress, which tears easily in half and falls away, to reveal a mechanical but highly feminine and stream-lined android.

"Future wife," she says mechanically.

He feeds finger bones to her champing, robotic maw. Each time she swallows a finger, smoke billows from her ears. I'm not sure if this is intended to be slapstick comedy or something more surreal.

"Eat! Eat, my lovely," the knight says and chortles, flicking his head back spiritedly. "You are so much better than the tin men of the ancient philosophers, animated only by so much chemical marriage. You have a working jaw! Why else does a man go hither to fight battles but to bring home a doggie bag of ears, noses, and fingers to feed to his future wife?"

A man in a rubber dragon suit shambles into the shot, looks around confused. The knight turns and shakes his head, glances quickly into the camera. The dragon man backtracks, removing himself from the frame.

Then we get to the part that is probably why they were showing us this movie in the court-room.

A midwife, hysterical, runs up to the knight, wailing. She's clutching a baby.

"The boy was born still! The boy was born still! There's no spirit within him!"

"Calm thyself, witch!" shouts the knight. He backhands the woman across the face and takes the dead babe from her grasp. "Future wife! Prepare thy womb!"

The future wife obliges, lying on her back and spreading her legs.

The knight crouches and forces the newborn inside the mechanical vagina. He pushes the crown all the way in and amber lights flash on the future wife's abdomen.

"What is a-happ'nin'?" the old midwife says, doddering and nearly swooning.

"The child is being returned to life. The future wife has a pure womb, a safe haven to incubate him further, rendering him whole. In time, he will be reborn."

"O forsooth?" the woman squeals. "Thank ye, Sir Chupalkin! The mother shall be very well pleased!"

"Mention it not! Tell no one what you have seen here! Go forth and sin no more!"

And then the film cut out and the lights came back on

43

in the room.

10

I had a dream recently. At first I could not recall very much of its content. But it so happens that something triggered me to remember the entire thing, in almost crystalline detail.

It started, or I became aware of the dream at first, in a mansion. Not opulent, not a mansion by any sane world standards. It was, in fact, an old factory warehouse that had been crudely renovated and filled with all manner of odd objets d'art. Most of these masterpieces were obviously salvaged junk: Oscar the Grouch-style trashcans forming elephant legs, pieces of car engines composing a startling simulation of a hi-fi, old pipe and wire bundled into the hair of pretty garbage ladies. There were about a dozen servants, each outfitted with Halloween-costume-shop-versions of their traditional attire. The maids wore skimpy, polyester skirts, wielding long unusable feather dusters. The butlers appeared to be extras from a Hammer horror film. And there was a brewer – a comically grotesque woman in her fifties dressed as a serving wench. But she carried herself in such a way that I knew she was in touch with the upper echelon. And it became apparent that things worked here in the opposite way. Servants were leaders. Scum was treasure. Brewers brewing not intoxication, but enlightenment. I knew that I could imbibe a beer that would make me wise if this woman would be generous enough to offer some to me.

She wryly smirked when she saw that I wanted to catch her eye. Wiggling her bulbous nose, she sidled up to me, rumpled bosom spilling out over the top of her bodice.

"I know what boys like," she said. But in my head, I knew she was not hitting on me. She was referring to that old song, but at the same time, she was letting me know that she understood what it was I sought.

From under her apron she produced a bottle. An old fashioned stopper on top. No label. A thick layer of tallow covering it.

I must have grimaced, because she saw the hesitation and pulled the bottle back.

"Johnny, are you queer?" she said.

I shook my head, but I was still reluctant to drink the strange brew she was offering me.

The bawdy woman cracked a snaggle-toothed smile. "Our lips are sealed." She mimicked turning a key on her closed mouth and tossed it away.

Me: When I drink that, what's going to happen to me?

Brewer: How should I know? You are your own man, aren't

46

you?

Me: I guess so. Sure. But what happens to others?

Brewer: None of my business.

Me: Aren't you curious?

Brewer: Not in the slightest. I don't have time for worrying about the aftershocks of Truth.

Me: Does anyone ever die from drinking your beer?

Brewer: Sometimes.

Me: They *die*?

Brewer: Shhh. Voices carry.

Me: Well, I don't want to die.

Brewer: I don't think you have much choice in the matter, darling.

Me: I want to know the truth.

Brewer: Then drink this. (Handing me the bottle.)

Me: (Accepting it, but looking it over carefully.) Where is it brewed?

Brewer: (Shrugging.) Hong Kong Garden.

Me: Chinese beer? Is it really Chinese?

Brewer: It's probably not. I doubt its name is really Charlie.

Me: Charles then… do beers have names? I mean, first names, in the way people have names.

Brewer: I don't know really. I don't think it matters. Would you drink a Willy or a Sam?

Me: Just as long as it's not a swill, I'll be happy.

Brewer: Hogs drink it, but so do brain scientists.

Me: Like water.

Brewer: More like *uisce beatha. Aqua vitae. Eau de vie.*

Me: So, there are immortal pigs running around.

Brewer: No, there are drunk pigs running around. Now drink the damn thing and join them.

I drank the damn thing, pulling away the stopper and guzzling it as quickly as I was able. I didn't taste anything at the time, but then later when I thought of it, it tasted like stale copper pipe kept in a cupboard at your grandmother's house behind an expired skull of some family pet that died before your conception. It's funny how in dreams you get not only the impression of something, but an impression of that impression, and you can dream the past at the same time, or even after, the present. I didn't taste it in the past, yet in the future I knew what it tasted like. That's crazy shit once you think about it.

In the right-center area of my brain, the potion deposited a parasite that formed a cyst of knowledge that grew so large so fast my mind popped like an overfilled balloon.

49

And it was then that I could see it: this brewer was no brewer. The Governor was no governor. And whoever was pulling the strings behind the scenes was being protected by his prominent puppet.

I woke up feeling as if it were three days ago. Or I woke up way in the future, in a court-room. Either way, I woke up and I understood what at first I would never have believed. We had been duped. And maybe Wilson, that head case, was right.

11

In high school they made us all read *Julius Caesar*. The text book had more footnotes explaining to us how to read the text than there was actual story. It got pretty boring toward the end. But the main thing I think we are all supposed to get out of *Julius Caesar* is how democracy is evil and monarchy is great. Shakespeare lived under a monarch, so he probably was scared to make the conspirators into heroes. But from a modern American high schooler's perspective, of course Brutus is the hero of the thing. He's bringing down a tyrant—a guy who had the power of a dictator and the popularity of a rock star. Even John Wilkes Booth got that much out of the story, and he was a goddamn actor so he'd probably read Shakespeare over and over until it sounded natural to him instead of stuffy and pompous and half-witted.

If you lived in a country, let's say—the size of a small city—, that was ruled over by a guy who no one elected, no one could check or override, and no one even knew what he looked like, would you be a Brutus or an Antony?

Now, the thing is, the conspiracy to make Brutus out to be a blustering thug did not end with Shakespeare. It was just getting started. Take a look at *Popeye*. After he got a makeover in the 60s, Bluto was Brutus. He was a real dick, too, always fucking with Popeye, who even someone in Shakespeare's time would have known to be the hero. Why change the already established Bluto's name, unless you wanted to impeach the credibility of the original Brutus, the emperor slayer? The fucking hippies were suddenly pawns of the monarchists, filling the cartoons and comics with propaganda.

And it got worse. The hippies were pushing evolution really hard. Archaeopteryx was their poster boy. They were getting that lizard-bird tattooed on their tits and sprayed on the sides of their microbuses. Two years after Darwin's masterwork sewed God's cocoon shut once and for all, they pulled that unholy fossil from the earth, seeming to prove his theories in a single stroke. But I told you before, Archaeopteryx was a dead end. It was his cousin that would have made Darwin proud. Just seeing a reptile with feathers was enough to make a Victorian era gentleman piss in his trousers. There can't be a God if there's something like that slithering around. What kind of villain would let that happen if he had the power to stop it? This is commonly known as The Problem of Archaeopteryx.

And the hippies didn't know what hit them when that beast returned from space, gliding down by his own power from the mothership. People were calling him Quetzalcoatl. Suddenly there were Aztecs taking to the streets in their head dresses and wooden armor. That's what I hated about the sixties. It wasn't a time for sane people. You couldn't simply go about your daily routine, go to work, go to the bowling alley, go to the grave of the elders, go to the Vanishing Temple. No, not without being assaulted by flying lizards in the name of progress, freedom, and being groovy.

And what if—what if that goddamn creature was still here among us? What guise would he need to take in order to avoid being put in a glass case in some museum? The form of a man. The form of a Governor?

And where would he hide his eggs? Incubators would be a dead giveaway. He'd have to get creative. Set up a lab. Put the eggs inside prostitutes. Keep them there until they ate their way free.

It all made perfect sense. Wilson was right. Even though what Wilson had claimed on the stand bore little resemblance to this truth I had uncovered, I knew he was using a form of code to get the information across to me without arousing the suspicions of the Winged Lizard Emperor. The ersatz Governor was among us in the courtroom—why not the hidden Governor? Only one way to draw him out....

12

As I stood up, the judge was mumbling some kind of instructions to the jury, which comprised sixty-six bag ladies between the ages of sixty-five and sixty-seven, each with her stroller or trolley full of collectable rubbish. The jury had the best seats in the house: the Naugahyde bench seats from various 1970s sedans.

"Now, ladies and crones of the jury, please understand that the last demonstration was only evidence in the same way that a fossil is evidence of evolution. I think you take my meaning, but in case you don't, I've written up note cards in Sanskrit and Phoenician, and I'll have the bailiff pass them to you now."

The gangly Arboghast stagger-stagger-crawled his way to the bench. His fists flicked down upon the stack of note-cards, like those of a praying mantis clutching at its delectable prey.

"Excuse me," I said softly several times as I tried not to trample the feet of those sitting in my row. Once I reached the aisle, the Arboghasts started closing in, so I didn't have much time. I walked right up to the Governor, or the man that we were told was the Governor, pointed my snub-nose right in his face and yelled, "*Sic semper Archaeopteryx!*"

I fired all six shots before the metallic talons bit into my shoulder, then my arms, driving me down to the floor. The Arboghasts clapped their crude shackles on me, making plastic clicks to one another, while in the background I could hear Wilson hooting, a mix of anxiety and happy surprise.

"He's dead! The Governor's been deaded!" cried some poor rube.

"He's not dead!" I said, face eating dirty shag carpet, tasting cat piss. "He's fucking flying around, laying eggs and shit!"

"Bailiffs!" the judge croaked "Haul this man to the Cannery!"

Something heavy and narrow and metal hit me in the back of the skull. A blunt head trauma, I think they call it. Blackness ensued.

13

Every inhabitant of Bum Town had heard of the Cannery. It's the kind of place that everyone said you never came out of once you went in. I always figured it was malarkey. But in a matter of moments I'd find out.

Upon coming around, the first thing I noticed was the smell of fish. The place hadn't been used in years, but the smell lingered there like a pervert in the women's room, staying behind to sniff the toilet seats.

The second thing I noticed was my hands were tied. A single lamp shone down from the high ceiling, lighting the space immediately surrounding me. I was in an old wooden

chair like the ones around my grandmother's dinner table. But instead of facing my grandmother eating her grits, I faced a man. He was just at the edge of the yellow light. A small man whose face I could not make out. A small man with a spectral appearance.

"Who the fuck are you?" I muttered, tongue slurring because it was only half awake.

"I might ask you the same thing," the guy said.

I told him my name. I had nothing to hide.

"Ah, that's what we thought. You've been a hard nut to crack. But even a toothless squirrel cracks a skull every once in a while." He rummaged in a green lawn and leaf bag and pulled out a portfolio. "You recognize this?"

"Huh?" I said.

"This was among the evidence in the Wilson case," he said. "I wonder if you wouldn't mind reading this." He held up a title page of a manuscript.

"*Clean Streets*," I said aloud. "By…"

"Go on, read it," the guy said, his lips curling down into a frown.

"No… that's not right." My name on the byline.

"Yes, I'm afraid it is right."

"I'm not a writer!" I protested.

"You may not be, but you were once." He put the paper back in the portfolio, then shot his hand back into the sack and came out with a paperback, which he tossed into my lap. It was a copy of *Abortionstein*. "You wrote this one under a pseudo-name."

"I don't understand. I have no idea what's going on."

"You think Quetzalcoatl is gonna let you run around Bum Town without paying the tribute?"

He stepped into the light, let it shine upon his face. When I got a better look at him, I saw that it was Wilson.

"What the fuck is going on here, Wilson?"

"I just want to know what you know, or what you think

you know, about the Governor," he said. He dropped the trash bag and pulled a pair of pliers from his pants pocket. Two more men approached. Both looked exactly like Wilson, but with different hairstyles. One had a mustache. One had a scar on his cheek. But they had on the gimp suits that Arboghasts wore, which really slimmed them down. And they made that squelching sound as they moved toward me. Each one had his chosen implement of information extraction held white-knuckled in one or the other of his mitts.

They spread my legs and tilted me back. Maybe this wasn't a wooden dinner table chair. And maybe I wasn't even in a cannery. Was it an operating room? The light was too bright in my eyes to really tell.

The first Wilson undid my fly, grabbed my dick with the pliers and pulled until I thought my brain was going to slide down into my gut. The screaming was unimaginable to me, so much so that my mind rejected the possibility that the noises were originating from me. They had to be torturing some other schmuck in the next room. It could not be me that was bawling.

As he yanked on my cock, one of the others took sheers and stuck one of the tips into my ass, cutting my asshole through. It felt like I was shitting glass. Fire and stabbing and scraping that would not subside. Somehow they had taken off my pants completely without my realizing it.

The other one stabbed me in the arm with a basting needle. Hooked up an IV of some kind.

And then it happened: the first Wilson slipped back. My dick had come free. But as I watched in abject revulsion, no blood gushed forth. There was merely a hole there, where it had been attached. It was a socket, the plug-in kind you can put on hoses.

The second Wilson cut the tissue between the socket and the asshole in a few snips. And then another Arboghast approached, but it had Chinese Charlie's head sewn onto an

awkwardly long, pale neck. His eyes stared toward me, yet the face showed no sign of recognition. He held a grayish alien baby, with an oblong head and dead, reptilian eyes. Its head lolled to the side, drooping like over-cooked broccoli stalks.

The first Wilson spread my legs even further, placing my feet in stirrups. I could feel two slimy hands inside.

"This won't hurt a bit," he assured me.

Truth to tell, pain does not adequately describe what I felt in that moment. But as the small being was shoved inside me and that odd feeling slid past my crotch and into my abdomen, my mind was really only fixed on one amazing fact, something that would never have occurred to me that morning before I joined the gallery for Wilson's trial. One revelation that I could not deny and that brought a strange sense of accomplishment to my fragile psyche:

I was going to be a momma.

Acknowledgements

G. Arthur Brown:

First Thanks to Sean Tigert, Casey Babb, and Matt Vest for reading this thing and telling me what's good about it.

Thanks go to Constance Ann Fitzgerald and Tiffany Scandal for "buying" *Abortionstein* in the High Concept Bizarro Workshop, as well as my sincerest apology for not being able to actually realize that concept into a full novel of its own (but who knows what the future holds?).

I'd also like to thank Jeremy Robert Johnson for his unbridled enthusiasm and eagle-eye, and Brian Keene for letting me drink his whiskey and sleep on his couch.

And an extra big THANX to Vince Kramer for being the best bud ever and letting me make his ex-toy room into my home.

The name *Wilson* is a reference to Pete Wilson, ex-governor of California, because I really liked the Disposable Heroes of Hiphoprisy's updated cover of "California Über Alles." Or it's a reference to one of either of two friends I had in high school—Matt or Brian—whom we called Wilson because they had the last name Wilson (very methodical, us). "Chinese Charlie" is the title of a Wrestling Superstars Before Surgery song. *Governor of the Homeless* is the title of one of the earliest Children of Science recordings, from the Casio keyboard/boombox days. The Street Cleaners were inspired by the Godflesh album title *Streetcleaner*. The term Arboghast was directly inspired by the Komeda song "Arbogast" for no particular reason. That song isn't about horrible, semi-human creatures at all. I could have just as easily decided to call them Flabberghasts, but I thought it sounded silly. "Flabbergast" is the superior song, by the way. There are a ton of New Wave song titles in there too, so have fun finding them all. I was listening to a lot of The Jesus Lizard, Big Black, Head of David, and Killing Joke when I wrote most of this, but I still think early 80s New Wave is pretty cool.

Psychedelic Horror Press:

Thanks to G. Arthur Brown (for your patience and commitment), Casey Babb, Sarah Kushwara, Jordan Krall, Jeremy Robert Johnson, Brian Evenson, John Skipp, Ross E. Lockhart, Brian Keene, Cameron Pierce, Brian Allen Carr, Gabino Iglesias, BizarroCon 2015 for giving us the idea and confidence to start this press, and everyone else who supports our press and other small presses.

G. Arthur Brown's Top Ten Works of Psychedelic Horror:

1. *Videodrome*
2. *Jacob's Ladder*
3. *Dark Property* by Brian Evenson
4. *Hausu*
5. *The Open Curtain* by Brian Evenson
6. *Carnivale* (TV)
7. *Teatro Grottesco* by Thomas Ligotti
8. *Santa Sangre*
9. *Phantasm*
10. *Beyond the Black Rainbow*

G. Arthur Brown, author of *Kitten* (New Bizarro Author Series) and the Wonderland Award-losing collection *I Like Turtles* (Strange Edge), has dedicated his life to being a weirdo. His fiction has appeared in such anthologies as *Bizarro Bizarro* (Bizarro Pulp Press) and *Axes of Evil* (Chupa Cabra House), as well as *Strange Fucking Stories II* (Strange House). He first saw *Videodrome* when he was eight years old and he was never the same again.

Made in the USA
Middletown, DE
08 August 2022

70790199R00045